Music on Mercury

By Jeff Dinardo
Illustrated by Dave Clegg

RED CHAIR
•PRESS•

Funny Bone Books

and Funny Bone Readers are produced and published by

Red Chair Press LLC   PO Box 333   South Egremont, MA 01258-0333

www.redchairpress.com

About the Author

Jeff Dinardo's books are filled with humor and silliness that captures a child's imagination. When not writing, Jeff runs a successful design firm specializing in textbooks for use in classrooms from K-8.

About the Artist

Dave Clegg lives and works on a small horse farm in north Georgia with his wife Lyn and their two children. All of Dave's work is done digitally on his computer. When he is not drawing, he can be found creating songs with his guitar or making robot sculptures!

Publisher's Cataloging-In-Publication Data

Names: Dinardo, Jeffrey. | Clegg, Dave, illustrator. | Dinardo, Jeffrey.
    Jupiter twins ; bk. 7.
Title: Music on Mercury / by Jeff Dinardo ; illustrated by Dave Clegg.
Other Titles: Funny bone books. First chapters.

Description: South Egremont, MA : Red Chair Press, [2019] | Interest age
    level: 005-007. | Summary: "Troop 552 is excited for the concert. But
    the lead singer gets sick and it takes quick action to save the
    music!"--Provided by publisher.

Identifiers: ISBN 9781634407526 (library hardcover) | ISBN 9781634407564
    (paperback) | ISBN 9781634407601 (ebook)

Subjects: LCSH: Twins--Juvenile fiction. | Mercury (Planet)--Juvenile
    fiction. | Outer space--Exploration--Juvenile fiction. | Concerts--
    Juvenile fiction. | CYAC: Twins--Fiction. | Mercury (Planet)--Fiction.
    | Outer space--Exploration--Fiction. | Concerts--Fiction.

Classification: LCC PZ7.D6115 Jum 2019 (print) | LCC PZ7.D6115 (ebook) |
    DDC [E]--dc23 | LCCN: 2018955672

Copyright © 2020 Red Chair Press LLC
RED CHAIR PRESS, the RED CHAIR and associated logos are registered trademarks
of Red Chair Press LLC.

All rights reserved. No part of this book may be reproduced, stored in an information
or retrieval system, or transmitted in any form by any means, electronic, mechanical
including photocopying, recording, or otherwise without the prior written permission
from the Publisher. For permissions, contact info@redchairpress.com

Printed in United States of America

0519 1P CGF19

CONTENTS

Meet the Characters

Trudy

Tina

Ms. Bickleblorb

Greta Gravel

CONCERT TIME

"**I** can't wait for the concert to start," said Trudy as she wiggled in her seat.

"We're lucky we all got tickets!" said her twin sister Tina, who was just as excited.

All members of Jupiter Troop 552 had gotten tickets to the concert on Mercury.

Their scout leader, Ms. Bickleblorb,
had brought them all in the space bus.
    She sat in her seat and wore a big set
of earplugs. She did not seem happy to
be there.

"*Greta Gravel and the Craters* are my favorite rock group!" said Trudy.

"Mine too," said Tina. "I love how they fly across the stage on their jet packs while they play."

Just then a green alien with big glasses slithered out on stage.

"Excuse me," he said nervously. "I have an important announcement to make."

"He's not part of the band," said Trudy. "I have a bad feeling about this."

The alien on stage looked out at the crowd.

"Greta Gravel is sick and cannot perform tonight," he said. "So the concert has to be canceled."

Everyone in the crowd grumbled and
started yelling.

Ms. Bickleblorb smiled happily.

"Okay, girls," she said. "Back on the space bus!"

"Not so fast!" said Trudy as she stood up and started walking toward the stage. "We came all this way. I'm not leaving until I know what's wrong."

"Uh-oh," said Tina, and she quickly followed her sister.

When they got behind the stage, the twins could see the rock band standing around their lead singer. Greta Gravel held her hands to her throat and looked glum.

"What's wrong?" said Trudy as she pushed her way into the group.

Greta

"Cherries," said the bass player. "There was a big bowl of them backstage, and Greta ate a handful."

"It must be an allergy," said Tina as she pulled a book out of her backpack.

"She is very allergic to Venusian cherries!" said the drummer. "It makes her throat swell up."

Jumping Jupiter," said Trudy. "Is it dangerous?"

Greta smiled and shook her head.

"No, she will be fine," said the drummer. "But it means she can't talk or sing until it clears up. And that could take a week."

Trudy and Tina were upset the concert would be canceled, but they were very sad for Greta.

"There must be something we can do," said Trudy.

Tina looked again in her allergy book. "Rest seems to be the best medicine," she said. "Unless, of course, anyone has a bottle of ice from the bottom of a deep crater?" Tina laughed at her own joke.

"What do you mean?" said Trudy.

"It says right here in the book," Tina said as she pointed out the page to her sister. "Frozen ice from the bottom of a crater will instantly cure a Venusian cherry allergy."

Trudy winked at her sister, then looked right at the band.

She asked the bass player and the drummer to borrow their jet packs, then she grabbed Tina.

"Don't cancel the concert," Trudy said as she blasted up into the air. "We'll fix this."

Tina gulped, then blasted off to follow her sister. "Wait for me!"

4 THE CRATER

Tina caught up to her sister.

"Where are we going?" she shouted.

Trudy pointed to the horizon and zoomed ahead.

"We are on Mercury," she said. "This planet has some of the biggest and deepest craters in the solar system."

Soon they saw an enormous crater on the planet's surface.

They both landed.

"What's that?" shouted Tina as she pointed to a giant creature sleeping by the crater's edge.

Trudy tiptoed over and patted the giant animal's sleeping snout.

"It's just a Long-Tongued Mercurian Lizard," she said. "They are pretty harmless, but their tongues are super sticky!"

Tina kept her distance. "I'm glad it's asleep," she said.

The twins looked over the crater's edge.

"It's so deep we can't even see the bottom," said Tina. "How do we know there is even ice down there?"

Trudy smiled.

"There is only one way to find out," she said as she blasted off and zoomed straight down the rocky side into the darkness below.

"Why can't I have a normal sister?" sighed Tina as she blasted off and followed Trudy into the deep unknown.

21

5 DOWN AND UP

Trudy and Tina flew down, down, down the crater's jagged side.

It was dark and spooky and getting very, very cold.

Finally, they saw the bottom and gently landed.

"Look!" shivered Trudy, and she pointed to a pile of ice. "I knew we would find it!"

Trudy pulled out a small bottle from her bag and scooped some of the ice into it.

"Now, let's get out of here!" she said.

Tina was looking at her jet pack with a worried face.

"I think we have a problem," she said as she looked at the gauge on the side. "I'm not sure we have enough fuel to fly us back out of here!"

Trudy looked at her gauge as well. "I'm almost out of fuel too," she said.

Tina shivered. "Now we are stuck down here forever."

Trudy just shrugged. "Not if I can help it," she said. "Do you still have your emergency food in your bag?" she asked.

"Of course," said Tina. "But how can you think about eating now?"

Trudy opened Tina's bag and pulled out a Raisin and Coconut Supreme Bar.

"Perfect!" Trudy said as she unwrapped it and started waving it high above her.

"What are you doing?" said Tina. "Have you gone crazy?"

"Here it comes!" Trudy said. "Quickly, grab ahold of me!"

Just as Tina grabbed her sister, a long, sticky tongue uncurled itself down the side of the crater.

"It's the Long-Tongued Mercurian Lizard," she said. "And it loves raisins almost as much as it loves coconut."

The long, sticky tongue curled around the girls. It grabbed them and the nut bar and pulled them into the air.

"Here we go!" said Trudy.

Up, up, up the side of the crater they went.

"Get ready to blast off when I say!" shouted Trudy.

Just as they reached the surface, they saw the lizard's hungry mouth wide open. It had razor-sharp teeth, and it was looking for its snack.

"Now!" shouted Trudy, and she and Tina hit the buttons that started the jet packs. The force pulled them off the sticky tongue.

They were free.

They flew off, leaving the lizard waiting for her snack.

"That was too close," Tina moaned.

Greta Gravel drank a glass of water filled with crater ice. She smiled as she rubbed her throat.

"Did it work?" asked the drummer.

"You bet it did!" Greta said. "Let's start the concert."

Trudy and Tina and all of Jupiter Troop 552 were invited to be on stage during the concert.

Even Ms. Bickleblorb was having a good time.

"This is the most fun I have ever had," said Trudy.

But something was bothering Tina.

"I think we have to do something after the concert," she said.

"What?" asked Trudy.

"We have to say thank you," said Tina.